The
HOMESTEADERS

PETER L. DIXON

To Sarah
Illustrations by Peter Catalanotto

Copyright © 1989, 1974 by Peter L. Dixon.
All rights reserved. Published by Scholastic Inc.
SPRINT and SPRINT BOOKS are trademarks of Scholastic Inc.
Printed in the U.S.A.
ISBN 0-590-35178-8

10   31   03 02 01 00

CHAPTER 1

Jamie Thompson had been in the plane for three hours. He wished he could take off his seat belt. But he knew his father wouldn't let him. Jamie and his mother and father were on their way to Alaska. They were flying in the family's Piper Cherokee. It was a floatplane that could land on water.

Jamie sat behind his mother and father. Behind Jamie were piled the tent and sleeping bags. And behind those were all the other things the Thompsons would need to start a new life.

Jamie was glad they would be landing soon. It had been a long, hard trip from California.

But at last it was almost over. For three days they had been flying north. They had stopped in Oregon and Washington for gas. They had spent the nights in motels near the small seaports. Last night they had stopped in Canada. Tonight they would be at their homestead. And they would be sleeping under the stars.

Jamie wondered whether he would like homesteading. When he had first heard that they were moving to Alaska to build a fishing camp, Jamie had liked the idea. But now he wasn't sure. He knew he was going to miss movies and television. He knew he was going to miss playing baseball.

To help pass the time, Jamie looked out of the window. Down below he could see nothing but trees. The forest looked wild and thick. Looking down at all the trees, Jamie knew there would be no one to play with and nothing to do. He knew he would miss his friends.

Jamie looked at his mother and father. His

mother was flying the plane. She sat in the copilot's seat. His father was looking over a map. Jamie wondered how many other people would give up a life in the city for the frontier of Alaska.

Jamie's father put the map away. He took the controls. Jamie's mother turned and said,

"There's our lake. We're going down."

Jamie looked down at the lake. The blue water sparkled. The sun was very bright. In this part of Alaska, daylight lasted 20 hours each day during the summer. Jamie wondered if he would be able to sleep while it was light.

Mrs. Thompson dropped the plane's wing flaps. She smiled and said, "We made it!"

Then Jamie's father banked the floatplane into the wind. He got ready to land.

"Is that our place?" asked Jamie as he looked at the lake.

"Yes," answered his father. "The whole west side of the lake. And 160 acres of land besides."

Looking out of the window, Jamie saw something move down by the water. He looked again and cried out, "Mom, look! A moose!"

By the lake three big moose lifted their heads. They looked up at the plane. When the plane skimmed over the water, the big animals ran for the woods. Hiding behind some trees, the moose watched the plane.

Mr. Thompson ran the plane across the lake. It came to a stop beside a bank. Mrs. Thompson took off her seat belt. She stepped out of the plane and jumped down into the water. The water came up to her waist. Jamie jumped down and turned toward the shore. His father tied a rope to the plane. He planned to tie the other end of the rope to a tree.

As Jamie walked toward shore, he looked around at his new home. He thought about the future. He wondered if he and his parents could make a good life here. It was almost 150 miles to the nearest town. As he looked at the forest, he wondered what dangers might be hidden among the trees. And then Jamie saw one of the dangers.

"Mom, Dad! A bear!" he screamed.

At the sound of Jamie's voice, the bear moved back into the woods.

CHAPTER 2

By suppertime, the Thompsons had unloaded the plane. Their tent was up. Mrs. Thompson had a cooking fire burning.

Jamie and his mother went fishing. There were lots of fish in the lake. In a few minutes Jamie had caught two big lake trout. He cleaned the fish, and soon they were cooking on the fire.

After dinner the family began to relax. Even though it was still daylight, it was time to sleep. The weather was so nice they decided to sleep outside. They crawled into their sleeping bags. And they slept.

When the four hours of darkness came, Jamie woke up. "Dad," he said, "something is wrong. I have a feeling we're being watched."

Mr. Thompson took his shotgun out of its case. He put it beside his sleeping bag. Then he told Jamie, "We'll keep watch. My turn first. I'll wake you in a few hours. Now try to go back to sleep."

An hour later Jamie was asleep, but so was his father.

The sun woke the Thompsons at four o'clock in the morning. Jamie was the first one to open his eyes. He looked across the meadow. He saw a family of deer. They were heading for the lake. Jamie watched them drink.

How beautiful, he thought. *I hope Dad doesn't have to hunt them.*

Jamie knew they were a long way from a supermarket. His father had said they would have to live off the land. And that meant hunting. But he hoped it didn't mean the deer.

Jamie was the first one out of his sleeping bag. He went down and checked on the plane. He wanted to make sure it was still safely tied. Without the plane there would be a 30-mile walk to a road.

The plane was all right. Jamie came back and started a cooking fire. He put on a pot of water. Soon his mother and father were up.

Jamie's mother started breakfast. And Jamie's father chopped firewood. Jamie ran to the lake. He wanted to try to catch some more fish.

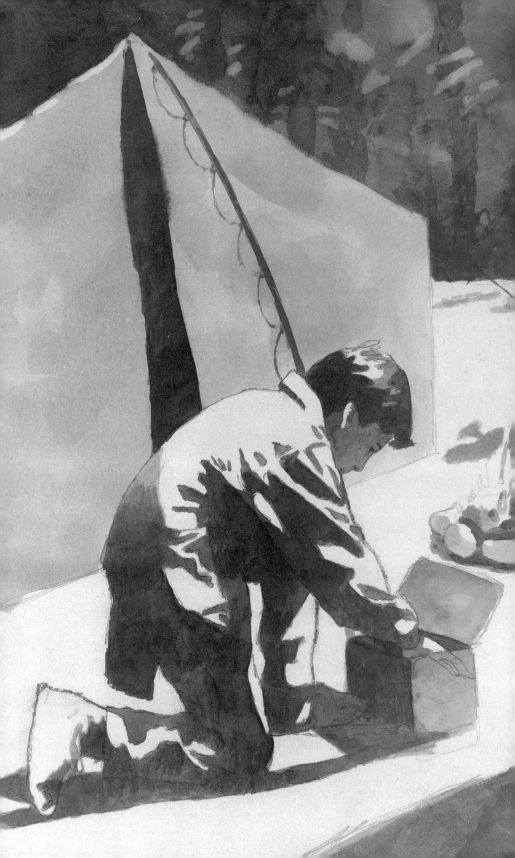

In the soft sand by the lake he saw a footprint — the biggest footprint he had ever seen in his life.

Jamie cried out, "Come quick!"

In a moment his mother and father were looking at the footprint. Mr. Thompson put his boot beside it. The print was at least two inches longer than his foot. "Whoever made that must be a really big man," he said.

"Looks like a moccasin print," said Mrs. Thompson.

"Indians!" said Jamie.

"Maybe, maybe not," said Mr. Thompson. "All the Indians I've seen around here are our size."

Jamie thought about the feeling he had had the night before.

"Someone was watching us," said Jamie. And he didn't like that idea. He promised himself to keep a close watch that night.

That night as the fire died down, the Thompsons got ready to turn in. Mrs. Thompson took the first watch. Then Jamie's father kept guard. And he didn't fall asleep. Just before dawn it was Jamie's turn. As the sun rose, Jamie looked across the lake. Suddenly he was wide awake. He saw what he thought was a giant man moving by the trees. When he looked again, the man was gone.

CHAPTER 3

Jamie climbed quickly out of his sleeping bag. He woke up his mother and father. He told them what he had seen. They all looked around the camp. Even though they had kept guard during the night, someone had been in their camp. Their clothesline was cut. And the ax handle was broken.

The family looked around for clues. They found another big footprint. Jamie became angry. He didn't like the tricks that were being played on them.

"We should set a trap," said Jamie's mother.

"A bear trap," said Jamie.

"No," said Mr. Thompson. "That would be

going too far. After all, our mystery man hasn't tried to hurt us. Tonight we'll be more careful. Two of us will stay up. That way we'll keep a good watch."

"We can tie cans to a string," said Jamie. "He'll trip over them and make a lot of noise. Then we can turn our flashlights on him."

"Good thinking, Jamie," said his mother.

The Thompson family worked together very well. That was the way they solved their problems. They had to find out who was coming into their camp. But that wasn't their only problem. They had to plant a garden. And they had to build a cabin before winter came. Alaska had a short summer. This meant the Thompsons had a lot of work to do in a short time.

They began work on the cabin that morning. Jamie's mother and father each carried a chain saw from the plane. Jamie carried the gas that the saws used. They spent the day sawing down trees. By the end of the day they had enough logs to start the bottom of the cabin. They planned to set the bottom logs in cement.

"I'll have to fly down to Anchorage soon for cement," said Jamie's father. "You and your mother will have to stay here alone for a day or so. How do you feel about that, Jamie?"

"We'll be fine, and you don't have to worry. We'll catch our man tonight for sure," said Jamie.

That evening Jamie and his father made a

noisemaker. They tied pans and empty cans to a string. They set their trap all around the camp.

During the short night, the Thompsons took turns staying up in pairs. They listened. They looked out into the darkness. But by dawn they hadn't seen or heard anything. The sun came up at four in the morning. Then all three slept. They wanted to rest two more hours before they began the day's work.

Jamie was the first to wake the second time. He looked over at the plane. What he saw made him jump and cry out. "The plane! It's going under!"

The floatplane was sinking into the lake.

Jamie and his parents ran for the lake. They found that one of the floats was flooded. The floats were like big skis. They were made of metal and were filled with air. They kept the plane on top of the water. Mrs. Thompson got the hand pump out of the plane. She and Jamie's father started pumping the water out.

Slowly the big plane righted itself. The float came up out of the water. There was a hole in the metal — a hole that had been made by a shot from a beebee gun.

"That does it!" said Mr. Thompson. "We are going to find out who is doing this! And we're not going to wait until tonight."

CHAPTER 4

The three Thompsons set out on a search around the lake. They had to find clues to who was trying to scare them away. Jamie's father carried his shotgun. And Jamie's mother carried a small .22 rifle.

As they reached the end of the lake, Jamie turned to look back at their camp. He saw someone coming out of the woods. Jamie pulled his father's arm and pointed. They watched the person for a moment. He was heading for their tent! Mr. Thompson turned around and ran for the camp. Jamie and his mother followed. *We'll get him now*, thought Jamie as he ran.

As they got closer to the camp, Mr. Thompson

stopped. Almost creeping, the family moved toward the tent. They could see that the man was huge. He was also old. He was carrying something on the end of a forked stick. He was looking so hard at what he was carrying that he didn't see the Thompsons.

"Just stop right there!" said Mr. Thompson. He pointed the shotgun toward the ground. It was a sign that he didn't mean to use the gun. Jamie figured that his father didn't think the old man was dangerous.

Now Jamie could see what was on the end of the forked stick. It was a swarm of bees! *What a dirty trick!* Jamie thought. *He was going to put the bees in our tent!*

Jamie's father took a step closer to the man. "Now, what is this all about?"

The stranger looked old enough to be Jamie's grandfather. His skin was like leather. His clothes looked homemade. His cold gray eyes moved from one Thompson to another. Then he spoke in a deep voice.

"Name is Yan. I live across the lake. Don't like kids, or neighbors. Just wanted to warn you." Yan glared at each of the Thompsons for a moment. Then he said, "You stay on your side of the lake. I'll stay on mine."

"OK, if that's the way you want it, Yan," said Jamie's father.

"That's the way I want."

Jamie's mother didn't like to let bad feelings stand between her family and a neighbor. "You're welcome at our homestead," she said. "But please leave your bees at home."

Yan said nothing. He looked at the bees.

"We haven't been on your side of the lake," said Jamie. "But you've been coming into our camp. Cutting down our clothesline. Breaking our ax handle. And trying to sink our plane."

"That's enough, Jamie," said his father.

Then Jamie's father told Yan, "We'll stay on our side. But I don't want you sneaking around here anymore!"

"I don't see why we can't be good neighbors," said Jamie's mother. "After all, there are only

four of us out here on all this land."

"Three too many," said Yan. "Don't need neighbors." Then Yan turned and walked away. He carried his bees with him.

"Just remember what I said," called Jamie's father.

Old Yan kept walking to the lake. When he reached some thick bushes, he pulled a canoe out of hiding. The old man climbed in and paddled across the lake.

"I hope that's the last we see of him," said Jamie.

"Well, I hope that's the last time we have trouble with him," said Jamie's mother.

"I think it will be," said his father.

CHAPTER 5

During the next week, old Yan stayed away. The hard work of building the cabin went on. Jamie helped with rolling the logs out of the woods. At the end of the week, there were enough logs to start the cabin. Jamie's father would have to fly south to Anchorage for cement and food.

The next day Mr. Thompson patched the hole in the plane's float. Then he climbed into the cockpit. The plane's engine roared. Mr. Thompson waved good-bye to his family. Soon the floatplane was skimming across the lake.

That night Jamie built a bigger fire than usual. When he crawled into his sleeping bag,

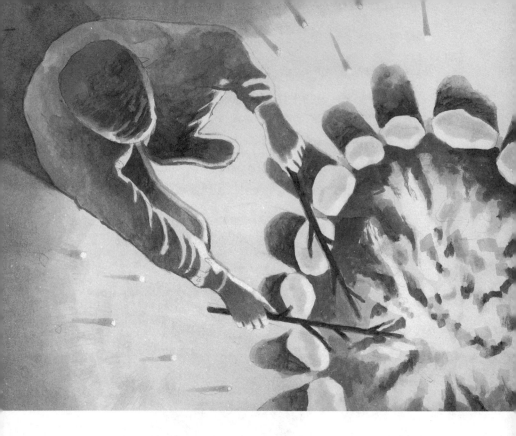

his father's shotgun was beside him. But nothing unusual happened during the night.

The next day Jamie and his mother started to work on their garden. The garden would be planted by the lake. There it would get the most sun. The seeds would have to be planted soon. But first the ground had to be plowed. The Thompsons had brought along a Rototiller. That would make the job easier. Jamie and his mother took turns running the Rototiller. The dark soil turned over easily. Jamie found many worms.

"All those worms mean rich soil," said Jamie's mother. "We'll have a good garden soon."

By the end of the day the garden was plowed.

Then they went over the broken ground picking out the rocks. They placed the rocks around the garden to make a low wall.

"We'll need to put a fence around the garden when the plants start growing," said Jamie. "If we don't, the animals will eat everything."

"You're right," said his mother. Then, seeing a worm, she said, "Why don't you try to catch a nice big fish for dinner?"

Jamie was tired of working in the garden. He was glad to go fishing. Leaving his mother in the garden, Jamie ran down to the lake.

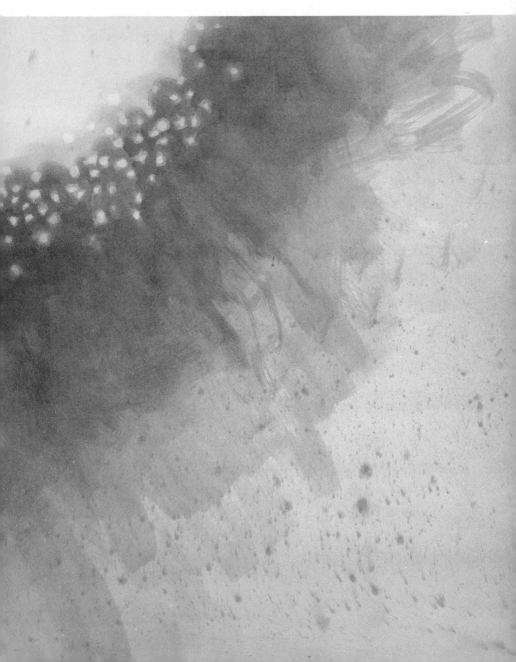

Jamie threw his fishing line into the water. Just then he looked across the lake and saw a large brown figure standing up in the bushes. It was a bear, a big one. For a long time Jamie watched the bear. The animal seemed to be eating berries. After a while the bear left the bushes and walked into the forest.

Seeing that the bear was gone, Jamie decided he wanted some berries. He knew the berries were on Yan's side of the lake. But he also knew his mother liked berries. Thinking of the jam she could make, Jamie headed for the rubber raft.

Without telling his mother, Jamie rowed across the lake. From the raft he watched the lake shore for the bear.

"I don't see that bear," Jamie said to himself. "But I'd better keep an eye out for old Yan."

When· he reached the other side of the lake, Jamie climbed out of the raft. He pulled the raft out of the water and ran for the bushes.

He pulled off a berry and tasted it. "Hey, these blackberries are sweet!" he said to himself.

Soon Jamie had his mouth full. Red juice dripped down his chin. When he could eat no more, he started putting the berries into his hat.

But when his hat was almost full, a dark shadow fell over him. Jamie turned around and looked up at old Yan. Yan was so tall and so broad he seemed like a giant.

The old man looked down at the berries Jamie had in his hat. "Them are my berries. You leave them be!"

"These berries are wild," said Jamie. "If the bears can eat them, so can we!"

Without a word Yan picked Jamie up and carried him to the raft. Then Yan dropped him into the raft.

"Stay on your side of the lake, you hear?" he said.

CHAPTER 6

With his hatful of berries, Jamie rowed back across the lake. He was mad at Yan. And he was mad at himself. He wished there had been some way of stopping Yan from putting him into the raft. *Well,* thought Jamie, *I guess I'll never be as big as Yan. I guess I'll have to stay on my side of the lake.*

In the garden Mrs. Thompson looked up to see Jamie rowing back. Jamie had not told her he was taking the raft. She hurried to meet him.

By the look on Jamie's face she knew that something was wrong. He told her about his trouble with Yan.

"You stay on our side of the lake," she told

him. "And that's an order!"

"I picked some berries for you, Mom," said Jamie. "And I would have had enough to make jam, but that old man came and stopped me."

Mrs. Thompson tasted one of the berries. "They are sweet," she said. "Thank you, Jamie. I think there are enough here to make a little jam. Help me carry some more rocks out of the garden. We can boil up the berries tonight."

"Boy, gardening is hard work," said Jamie. "Fishing is easier."

"But we can't live on fish alone," said Jamie's mother.

"How do you suppose old Yan lives?" asked Jamie. "I bet he doesn't have a garden. I bet he lives like a bear and sleeps all winter!"

Jamie and his mother laughed and talked as they worked.

On the other side of the lake the brown bear was again picking berries. And on the other side of the tall bush was old Yan. He too was picking berries.

When they both moved on to some low bushes, the bear and the man saw each other. The bear growled.

Yan knew that if he made a lot of noise the bear would run away. Yan shouted as loud as he could, "Get out of here!"

But the bear wasn't finished eating. It didn't move. It just growled back at Yan.

Yan walked closer to the bear and shouted again, "Get out of here!"

In answer, the bear swung a paw at the old man. The bear's sharp claws raked across Yan's chest.

Yan pulled away. But the claws had cut deep. He saw blood flowing from the cuts. He knew he was hurt badly. Yan backed away before the bear had a chance to claw again. The bear didn't follow Yan. It began eating berries again.

Yan ran for his cabin. The old man stumbled and fell three times before he reached it. He had lost a lot of blood and he was weak.

Inside the cabin he fell again. He no longer had the strength to get up. He needed help. And the only help was across the lake. So Yan crawled to where he kept his rifle. With his last bit of strength, Yan fired three shots through the roof. Then he dropped the rifle. His eyes closed. And he passed out.

CHAPTER 7

Bang! Bang! Bang! Yan's three shots were heard across the still lake. Jamie and his mother looked up from their gardening.

"What was that?" asked Jamie's mother.

"Trouble!" answered Jamie. "Three shots means someone needs help."

"It must be old Yan!" said Mrs. Thompson.

"Do you think it's a trick?" asked Jamie.

"I don't think Yan would do that. He wouldn't call for help unless he really needed it."

Jamie looked up at his mother. Mrs. Thompson knew there was only one thing to do. They must cross the lake and find out what was wrong.

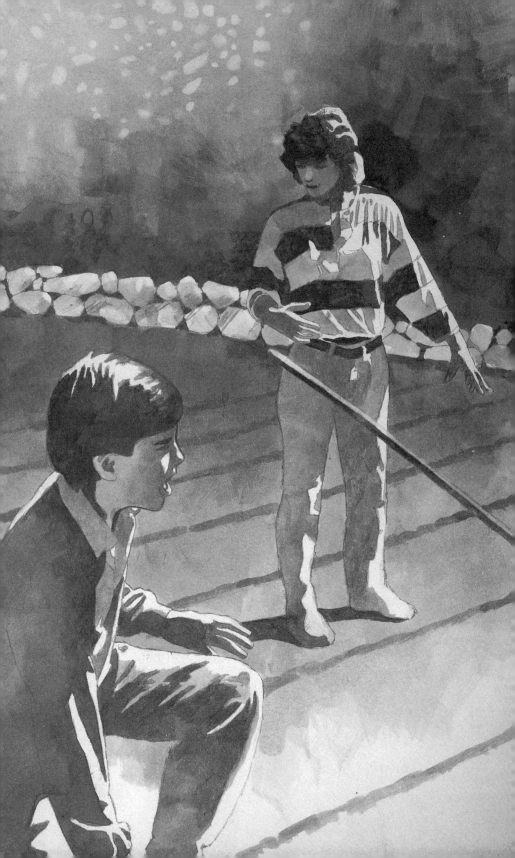

"Jamie, run and get the first-aid kit," said Mrs. Thompson. "We're going over there."

Jamie ran to the tent. He found the first-aid kit. Then he and his mother ran for the rubber raft.

Soon she and Jamie were rowing across the lake. Jamie suggested that they start looking for Yan by the berry patch.

"That's the last place I saw him," said Jamie.

At the berry patch Jamie and his mother found the bushes crushed. Then they saw the bear's footprints. And a little later Jamie found blood on the ground. It was easy to guess what had happened to Yan. But where was the old man now? And where was the bear?

Before they could take another step, they heard a slow growl behind them. Jamie and his mother stopped. When they turned around, they saw what they had expected. The bear! And it was coming toward them.

Jamie knew they couldn't outrun a bear. They had to find another way to get away.

Mrs. Thompson wished she had brought the shotgun along. But she hadn't.

The bear kept coming. When it was about ten yards from them, it stopped. It stood up on its back legs. It growled again, but didn't move. Jamie had seen bears in the zoo, but never this close. Jamie knew his mother was scared. And he was scared, too.

Jamie looked around. He and his mother tried to figure out a way to escape.

About ten yards to the right of Jamie was a big boulder. It was about ten feet high. Next to it was a small boulder. It was about two feet high. Jamie's mother looked at the big boulder closely. From where she stood, it looked very smooth, smooth enough so that a bear couldn't climb it. If only she and Jamie could get on top of it.

"Jamie," she whispered.

Jamie's eyes blinked at her.

"You see that big rock?"

"Yes," said Jamie.

"That's our only chance. We've got to get on top of that rock. Do you think you can climb it?"

Jamie moved his eyes slowly over to the rock. But before he could answer, the bear came charging.

"Run!" cried his mother.

Without thinking, Jamie headed for the rock. His mother ran in front of him. She jumped up on the small boulder. Then she made it to the top of the bigger one. Jamie tried to follow her. He made it to the smaller one. But he couldn't climb up the bigger one. He could feel the bear getting close.

"Jamie, take my hand!" cried his mother.

Again without thinking, Jamie found himself moving. But this time he was being pulled up. He was being pulled away from the bear.

47

CHAPTER 8

The bear tried to climb up after Jamie. But the rock was too smooth. There was no place for the bear to hang on with its claws. It looked up and growled at Jamie and his mother.

"I think we're safe!" said Jamie.

"We'll have to stay here until we are sure he is gone," said his mother. "Then we'll find Yan."

The bear growled at them for another ten minutes or so. Then it went away.

Jamie and his mother stayed on the rock. Twenty more minutes went by. They had to be sure the bear was gone. When they felt it was safe, they climbed down.

"We have to find Yan," said Jamie.

"I hope he is still alive," said Mrs. Thompson.

Jamie and his mother went back to where they had found the drops of blood. They followed the red marks through the woods. Jamie kept an eye out for the bear. But the bear seemed to be gone.

The trail of blood led them to Yan's cabin. It was an old one. It looked as if it was ready to fall down. Slowly Jamie's mother pushed open the door.

On the floor lay old Yan. Beside him Jamie saw the rifle. His mother ran over to the old man. Yan was still breathing. But he was breathing very weakly. They could see he had lost a great deal of blood.

"He needs a doctor right away," said Jamie's mother. "Jamie, you have to go back to the camp to call for help. Do you think you can make it?"

"Yes," answered Jamie. "But I won't go the way we came. The bear might still be out there. To be safe, I'll find another way back to the raft."

"Good," said his mother. "Try to radio for a plane. There may be some pilot nearby. Tell whoever you reach that we need help. That's the only way we can get a doctor."

As fast as he could, Jamie found another way to the lake. When he reached the raft, he felt safer. Now he didn't have to worry about the bear.

49

Jamie rowed back across the lake. At the tent he found their small portable radio. Jamie turned the radio set on.

The two-way radio wasn't powerful. It could only send signals a few miles. Jamie hoped that someone would be listening. He pushed the

"talk" button. Then he said the code word that fliers used to call for help. "Mayday . . . this is a Mayday!"

There was no answer.

Jamie tried again and again.

Several miles away a pilot flying north

thought he heard a "Mayday." He tuned his radio. Then he heard Jamie loud and clear. The pilot radioed Jamie that he understood. With his more powerful radio he would call for help and a doctor.

Sixty miles to the south of the homestead, Jamie's father was flying home. He heard the message that was passed on from Jamie.

Jamie's father sent his own message saying that he would be home soon. He also said that he would be within radio range in half an hour. Jamie's father pulled the plane's throttle full

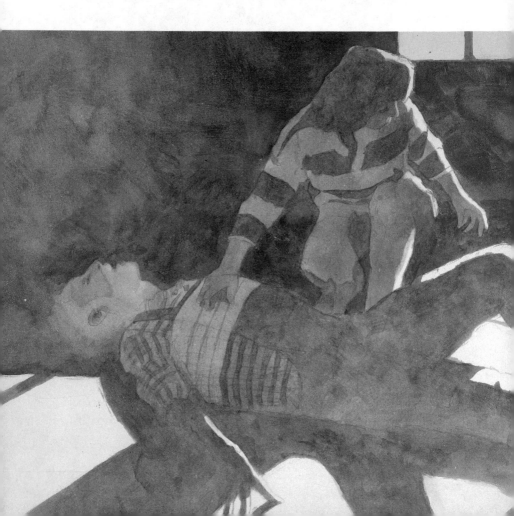

forward. The plane raced through the skies for the homestead.

Across the lake the brown bear began sniffing the ground. The bear sniffed at the blood. Then it followed the trail of blood to Yan's cabin.

Inside, Jamie's mother had just finished putting a bandage on Yan's deep cuts. The bleeding had stopped, but he still needed a doctor. Then she heard a strange snorting noise outside. She looked out the door. Coming straight for the cabin was the large brown bear.

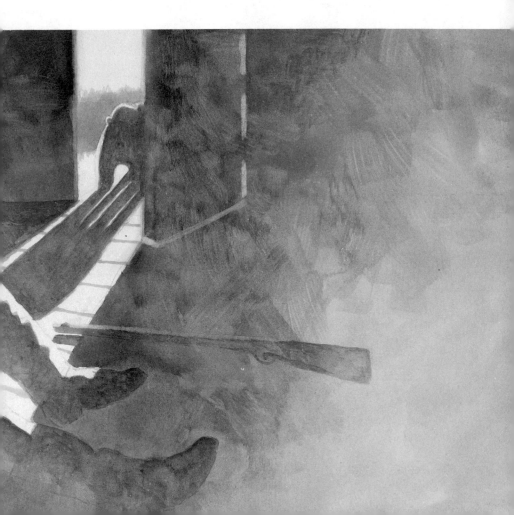

CHAPTER 9

The bear headed for the cabin. Jamie's mother slammed the door and locked it. She could hear the bear sniffing just outside the door. Then the bear started banging against the door. The old wooden boards rattled. She knew it was only a matter of time until the bear broke the door down.

Across the lake, Jamie heard his father's voice coming over the small radio. Mr. Thompson was within radio range now. Jamie told him what had happened. His father radioed back, saying he would be landing soon.

"Come as fast as you can," said Jamie. "Old Yan has lost a lot of blood."

"I'll be down soon," answered his father. "And Jamie, you'd better keep an eye out for that bear. You never know. It might come back."

"I understand, Dad," answered Jamie.

The bear was sniffing around Yan's cabin. He was looking for a way to get inside. The large animal made a circle around the cabin. When it returned to the front door, it clawed at the boards again.

Jamie's mother looked for a way to defend herself. The bear gave the door another big smack. One of the boards cracked.

She stepped back. Then she saw Yan's rifle lying on the floor. She picked it up. She looked to see how many bullets were in it. There were only two. And there wasn't time to look for more.

The bear gave the door another whack. A second board split. Mrs. Thompson pointed the gun. She fired through the door. The bullet nicked the bear. The big brown gave a cry and backed away. Then it turned to attack the door again.

At the homestead Jamie heard the single gunshot. "What's going on over there?" Jamie said to himself. After thinking for a moment, he knew the answer. His mother must be in trouble.

"I have to call Dad," said Jamie to himself. "Then I'm going across the lake."

In the air, Jamie's father was nearing the homestead. He could see the lake. Then he

heard Jamie's message. He told Jamie to head across the lake.

"And take the shotgun, Jamie!" said his father.

"Right, Dad," answered Jamie. "And please hurry!"

"I'm coming down now."

Jamie ran to the tent and got the shotgun. Then he ran for the lake. Jamie started rowing as fast as he could.

Jamie's mother waited for the bear. The door was breaking apart. She had one shot left. She had to wait for the bear to rush in. That one shot would have to stop the big brown. If she didn't kill it, it would surely kill her and Yan.

The bear kept hitting the door. More and more cracks appeared. Then from the sky came a low sound. It gave Mrs. Thompson hope. It was a plane's powerful engine.

From the plane Mr. Thompson looked down. He saw Jamie rowing as fast as he could. Jamie waved once to his father. He kept on rowing. His father banked the plane into the wind. Then he began his landing.

The plane and the life raft reached the shore at the same time. In less than a minute Jamie and his father were running for Yan's cabin. As they neared the cabin, they saw the bear clawing at the door.

Jamie's father grabbed the shotgun from Jamie. But as he raised the gun, the bear

knocked down the door and charged inside.
Suddenly a shot rang out from inside the cabin.
Then there was silence.

Jamie and his father ran toward the cabin.
But before they reached it, the bear came out.
The big brown bear twisted. Then it fell to the
ground. The bear was dead.

Jamie and his father ran inside. Jamie's
mother was holding Yan's gun. She was shaking.
But there was a smile on her face.

It took all three Thompsons to carry Yan to the plane. Jamie's father had to fly him to a doctor. Jamie's mother went along too.

"We can handle bears," said Jamie's father. "And we'll handle other problems too. I think we're going to make it all right."

Jamie thought for a moment. "You know, I think we're going to get along with Yan, too. He'll have to agree that sometimes it's nice to have neighbors."